JEREMY AND THE PUDDLE

Christopher Hobbs

faber and faber

LONDON · BOSTON

First published in 1990
by Faber and Faber Limited
3 Queen Square London WC1N 3AU

Photoset by Parker Typesetting Service Leicester
Printed in Belgium by Proost International Book Production, Turnhout, Belgium

British Library Cataloguing in Publication Data

Hobbs, Christopher
Jeremy and the Puddle.
I. Title
823'.914[J]
ISBN 0-571-15249-X

Jeremy was an awful child whose greatest joy
was puddle-splashing. When out with his mother
in the park, Jeremy would look out for the biggest,
dirtiest puddles and leap right into the middle.

SPLAT!

His mum's tights were ruined again.

One damp and dreary day Jeremy spotted the
perfect puddle, huge and round and muddy.
Cautiously creeping from his mother's side,
he drew a breath and leaped . . . and disappeared!

Down through greenish gloom he
dropped into a tunnel carved
from dripping stone.
Silence . . .

A rumble of tiny feet.

Suddenly Jeremy was surrounded by beady-eyed creatures.

'We are the Lemmings,' they said, 'What are you?'

'Jeremy,' said Jeremy.

'We've never heard of a Jeremy,' they cried,

'but come with us!' . . .

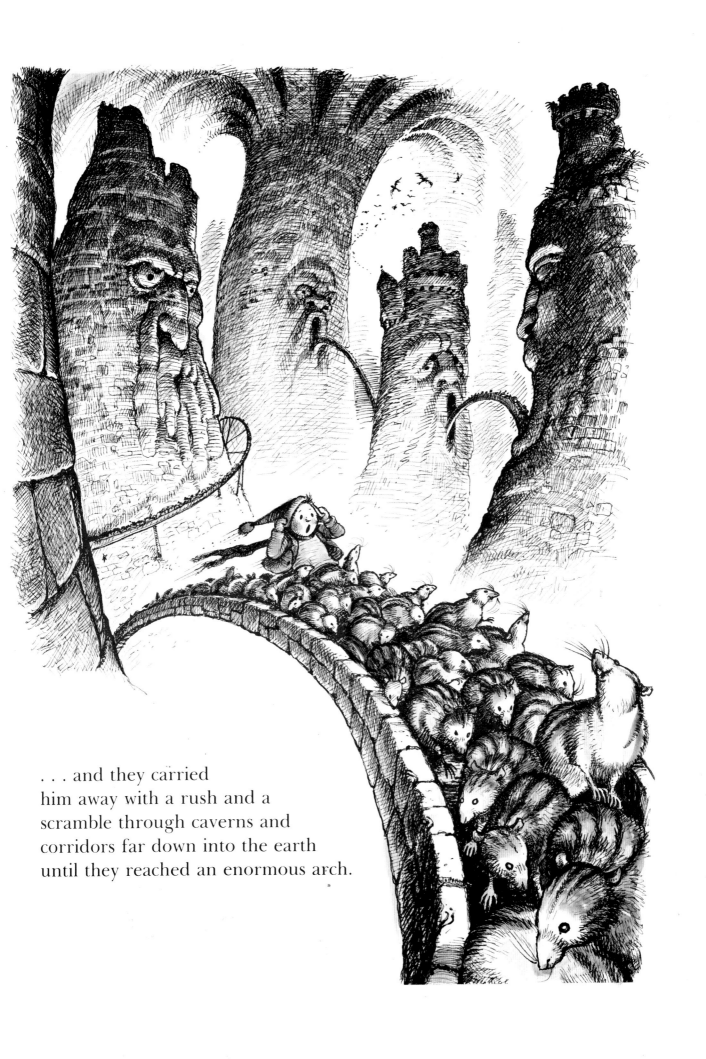

. . . and they carried
him away with a rush and a
scramble through caverns and
corridors far down into the earth
until they reached an enormous arch.

Beyond lay nothing
but a dreadful drop. Jeremy
cried 'Stop!', but the Lemmings
poured over the edge in a furry
wave, sweeping him, shrieking,
with them.

However . . .

A Something with enormous claws
swept Jeremy to safety leaving the splash
of doomed Lemmings far behind.

Low over a subterranean sea they flew
towards a tiny pink island. At its
centre stood a temple of green
porcelain hung about with little bells,
and on the peak of the roof, balanced
on a gilded rod, a golden fish swung
like a weathercock.

They landed with a bump and Jeremy turned to
see a solemn Secretary Bird.

'Card please,' it said. Obediently Jeremy
produced a crumpled Krunchy cereal voucher
from his pocket.

'No good at all,' said the Bird.

The temple doors flew
open revealing a lift and
Jeremy and the Bird
descended . . .

Below was a chaos of Newts and Lizards staggering under piles of paperwork. Dust filled the air from toppled towers of files.

'The Records Department, centre of the Nation,' said the Bird proudly. 'Come on!'

In his office, he consulted his computer for records of Jeremy.

'Not there!' he shrieked. 'Why . . . you must be from OUTSIDE!
For a thousand years we have been trapped down here trying to escape; locked behind all the shiny surfaces in your world, forced by an ancient punishment to provide you with reflections by mimicking your every movement. Now YOU pop through with the answer; if you got in you must know how to get out. The Emperor will make me rich!'

Bristling with triumph the Bird
locked Jeremy in a little library
and bounded away, hooting with
joy. Left alone, Jeremy built a
staircase of books and escaped
through the narrow window into
a strange garden.

Vellum trees with paper fruit stood in parchment tubs under a green and watery sky.

'HELP!' cried a Newt from another window in the leatherbound wall. With his scarf, Jeremy pulled him free.

'Thanks. I'm Fig Newton. I was caught cleaning the inside of a mirror at the wrong time. Someone from OUTSIDE saw my face instead of his own in the reflection, so of course I was thrown into prison. I'd have been sent to the Maggot Farms for sure,' said Fig.

Jeremy shared his only boiled sweet with him and they fled.

'I have a friend called Lug who'll feed us,'
said Fig as they rushed down stony corridors
to the Imperial kitchen.

Amidst the smoky clamour, Fig's friend
offered them the tastiest snacks: beetle vol-au-
vent and maggot pie.

'But I want a burger,' cried Jeremy in disgust.
An awful silence fell.

'WHO SAID THAT?' bellowed the Master
Cook as he rolled, huge and toadlike, through
the steam towards them.

Fig grabbed Jeremy and they ran until, quite breathless, they burst through an archway and stopped astounded before the Imperial Mirror Maze.

A city of little grey cubicles spread to the horizon. Gleaming above were the coral towers and pearl-hung roofs of the Emperor's Palace.

Suddenly, with eerie howls, a Soldier Crab burst
from behind a wall and rushed at Fig and Jeremy.
They fled and, slipping into the nearest cubicle,
closed the door quietly behind them.

Before a large mirror sat a Frog upon an ottoman, fanning his toes. A wardrobe to one side bulged with costumes and masks, and the back wall was decorated as a suburban hallway, complete with umbrella stand and framed print.

Above the mirror a sign flashed on:

'Amelia Bloggs: purple hat; orange coat and green umbrella.' Leaping to his feet, the Frog flung on a mask and orange coat. As Amelia Bloggs appeared beyond the glass, the Frog supplied her reflection, imitating every move she made until she walked out of view. Exhausted, he sank upon his ottoman and turned . . .

'By my toes!' he screamed. 'Intruders!' and he lunged at Fig and Jeremy. Masks went flying, coats fell down and the umbrella stand fell straight through the mirror.

From the black depths beyond there appeared a terrible golden mask with huge watery eyes. Smoke poured from its mouth. It spoke:

'WHO DARES MEDDLE WITH THE EMPEROR'S MIRRORS?'

The Frog squealed and fled, closely followed by Jeremy and Fig.

Out they ran, straight into the arms of the Secretary Bird and a posse of Soldier Crabs who marched them off towards the Palace.

In the Throne Room the Emperor sat surrounded
by his Court. His robes were heavy with jewels,
but his golden mask was the same as the one in
the broken mirror.

'So,' hissed the Emperor, 'you know the secret
of crossing between the worlds.'

Jeremy shook his head.

'Tell me, or your friend shall go to the
Maggot Farms,' howled the Emperor.

Jeremy hesitated.

'If Fig could go home, p'raps I would tell,' he
said.

The Emperor growled, but signalled for Fig's
parents to be found. Soon they arrived and
reclaimed their errant child.

'Now,' purred the Emperor, 'tell me.'

'I'm hungry,' pouted Jeremy.

The Emperor blinked an eye and a feast appeared, borne by beautiful Lobsterettes – dragonfly fricassee, worm-in-the-hole, boiled jellyfish.

'Oh, no!' thought Jeremy, 'I'll starve.'

But then he noticed on the floor before him a row of shiny, coloured sweets. He grabbed and pulled . . .

. . . but they were the jewels on the Emperor's robe! Down came robe, mask and all, revealing a big crystal bowl containing a golden carp. It teetered on its pedestal and CRASH! smashed to the floor.

'But it's just a goldfish,' said Jeremy, amazed.

With a roar the lights went out and the whole Court rose and rushed at Jeremy. Out of the Throne Room, down deeper and ever damper tunnels, he ran until at last he left the pursuit behind.

There in a gloomy cavern he sank exhausted and in tears.

'I want my mum,' he sniffed and no sooner had he said
it than he saw her reflected upside down in the pool at his
feet. He stretched towards her . . .

. . . and fell right through . . .

. . . out of the puddle in the park.

  'Look at you, Jeremy, you're soaked, and so are my
tights,' moaned his mother, hauling him from the pool.
Crossly she pulled him towards the park gates.

But Jeremy was VERY careful not
to step in the puddles on the way.

PRINTED IN BELGIUM BY

proost

INTERNATIONAL BOOK PRODUCTION